CLIFFHANGERS
Runaway Bus!

ERIC WEINER

BERKLEY BOOKS, NEW YORK

RUNAWAY BUS!

A Berkley Book / published by arrangement with
the author

PRINTING HISTORY
Berkley edition / September 1996

The Putnam Berkley World Wide Web site address is
http://www.berkley.com

ISBN: 0-425-15380-0

BERKLEY ®
Berkley Books are published by The Berkley Publishing Group,
200 Madison Avenue, New York, New York 10016.
BERKLEY and the "B" design
are trademarks belonging to Berkley Publishing Corporation.

PRINTED IN THE UNITED STATES OF AMERICA

10 9 8 7 6 5 4 3 2

CHAPTER 1

I'M GOING TO CATCH THE BUS! I'M GOING TO CATCH the bus!

As I run down my driveway, I keep saying this to myself.

I can't believe it. Today I'm going to catch the bus!

My parents have a nickname for me. They call me Mr. Late. They say I'm ten minutes late for everything.

I hate that nickname, but it's true. I *am* late a lot. I don't know why. I mean, I always *think* I'm going to be on time. I'm as surprised as anybody when I look at my watch and see how late it's getting.

But right now I'm not Mr. Late. I'm Mr. Early. I just reached the end of my driveway and it's—

Let's see—

Only ten after seven! Five whole minutes before the school bus gets here!

I swing my skateboard like a bat. "Yesss!"

My parents work in New York City. That's just over the George Washington Bridge from my hometown of Elmsford, New Jersey. Mom and Dad leave early to beat the morning traffic. So if I *miss* the bus . . .

If I miss the bus, things get hairy.

I have to bike to school. And I nearly get run over because I have to ride on the busy streets. Then I get to school around forty minutes late, all worn-out and sweaty.

That isn't even the bad part. Next I have to beg Ms. Marville, my sixth-grade homeroom teacher, not to report my tardiness to the principal's office.

Then Ms. Marville reports me anyway. And the principal's office calls and leaves a message on our answering machine. Something like, "He did it again."

I erase that message before my parents hear it, of course. But I still feel rotten.

But not this morning. This morning I have five—

Well, four, now.

Four whole minutes before the school bus gets here. I don't have time to relax, though. 'Cause I have to do my math take-home test.

Oh, boy. How could I leave the test until this morning? I mean, this test is EXTREMELY IMPORTANT. Mr. Himmelfarb says the take-home is worth 20 percent of our entire grade!

I'm a big stupid jerk, that's all there is to it. But if I stay calm, I think I can get out of this. There are thirty problems on the test. I did one last night. I can do another one right now before the bus comes. Then I figure I can do six or seven on the bus. And then I have my whole lunch period to finish. Perfect.

I unzip my backpack and take out my . . .

Take out my . . .

Uh-oh.

Where is my math test?

CHAPTER 2

I'M RUNNING AGAIN. RUNNING LIKE A BAT OUT OF YOU know what. Up the driveway. Up, up, up.

It's October—and very cold. The icy air cuts my lungs with every gasp.

Why do we have to have such a long driveway?

I've got two minutes to find my math homework and get back to the end of the drive or I miss the bus.

Of course, maybe the bus will be late.

Fat chance.

Mr. Dickerson, our bus driver? He's Mr. Always-Right-On-Time. He arrives every morning at 7:15 on the dot. And if you're not right there waiting, he drives off.

Okay, first I have to punch in our security-alarm code. Otherwise, in about thirty seconds, the alarm will blast so loud it breaks your eardrums.

I'm scared of burglars. But I'm more scared of this

alarm. At night, Dad puts it on and you can't go downstairs. Except I always forget and go down for a glass of milk and—

It's terrifying, let me tell you.

I punch in the numbers. I'm not going to tell you *what* numbers, of course. I'm not that stupid.

I unlock the door and race into the house.

Up the stairs.

ONE MINUTE LEFT!

You know, it's a good thing I'm running so fast, because I have this thing where I hate being in the house all alone. I get scared.

I know. I'm twelve years old. I shouldn't get scared so easy. But what can I tell you? When I'm alone in the house, I start thinking I'm not alone, if you know what I mean. Like maybe some burglar crept inside and figured out how to turn off the alarm and is waiting to pounce on me.

There's my math take-home test, sitting on my desk. Right where I didn't finish it last night. I grab the papers, stuff them into my backpack, then turn to run back out of the room as—

Somebody lets out this horrible SCREAM!

CHAPTER 3

I SCREAM, TOO. I NEARLY FALL FLAT ON MY FACE I'M SO frightened.

Then it hits me.

Whoever is screaming, they're screaming awfully long and awfully loud.

Now I know who it is. I mean, *what* it is. It's the burglar alarm. I punched in the wrong numbers after all.

I don't have time to call the burglar-alarm company and tell them it's a false alarm. All that will happen is that some security guard will come to the house, see that everything is fine, and shut off the alarm. No biggie.

Right now, I have to make the bus. So I race back down the stairs, taking them two and three and four at a time.

Four at a time? That's called falling. Nearly broke my neck, too.

So now I'm limping out the front door and the alarm is going like a maniac. And finally I get back to the front of the drive. I take a deep breath and look at my watch.

Seven twenty-one.

My heart sinks all the way down to my sneakers.

I give out a low moan.

Mr. Late has struck again.

I missed the bus.

CHAPTER 4

I MISSED THE BUS.

I missed the bus.

I missed the bus.

I can't believe it, not even after I say it to myself over and over. I have this awful feeling like someone kicked me in the stomach. Nooo! That Dickerson! He didn't even honk!

Then I hear someone call my name.

Mr. Hatchett, my new neighbor, hurries down the street. He's smiling, but he looks tense. He has his little daughter with him. Something's up, I can tell. And I'm not in the mood for anything.

"Hey, there, Fred," Mr. Hatchett calls.

I'm still breathing really hard from running up and down the driveway. It's a little hard for me to talk. So I just wave.

"Uh, Freddy, I don't know if you've met—this is my daughter, Sam."

"Hi, Sam," I say.

I'm thinking, *Sam?* But I don't say anything. Maybe it's short for Samantha. Or else, Mr. Hatchett has a *weird* sense of humor.

"Say hi, Sam," Mr. Hatchett tells her.

Sam doesn't say hi. She has big thick glasses like her dad. She's clutching a lunch box and this raggedy brown rabbit doll. She looks scared.

Frowning, Mr. Hatchett stares up at our house, where the alarm is still WOO-WOO-WOOING!

"Everything okay?" he asks me.

"Oh, yeah," I say. "Sorry about the noise. That alarm is busted or something. The man is on his way to fix it."

"Ah," Mr. Hatchett says. "So. You're waiting for the bus?"

"Yeah," I say glumly. "But I have a long wait. It won't be coming till *tomorrow* morning. I just missed it."

Mr. Hatchett goes bug-eyed. He whips his wrist around and studies his watch. "Doesn't the bus come at seven-fifteen?" he asks.

"That's right."

"Well, it's only ten after."

"Your watch is slow," I say with a shrug.

Mr. Hatchett stares at his watch. Then he bends down and turns his daughter's arm so he can see her Mickey Mouse wristwatch.

"I think *your* watch is fast," he says.

I feel a tiny bit of hope. But how . . . ? I mean, I can believe my watch is fast. But what about all the clocks in my house? They all said—

Then I remember. Last night Mom said she had a special plan for making me on time. Now I know what the plan was. She must have set my watch and the clocks in the house ten minutes ahead!

"Wow!" I say, smiling. "That's great news!"

So now I'm thinking I can catch the bus and finish my math take-home test after all. Everything is going to work out. I feel like hollering.

Then Mr. Hatchett says, "So here's the deal, Fred."

Mr. Hatchett works on Wall Street. Dad says that every day he makes deals worth millions. I believe it, too. Because when he talks to you, he's always saying, "Here's the deal." Like he's trying to sell you something.

He sure sells me. He talks really fast and in about two seconds he gets me to promise that I'll sit with Sam and make sure nothing bad happens to her.

I want to tell him that I can't sit with her because I have this math take-home test. I get my mouth open to tell him, but he turns to Sam and says, "See? Freddy would *love* to sit with you."

Sam tugs on her father's arm. "You promised!" she whispers.

"I promised *what*?" asks Mr. Hatchett.

"You promised you would drive me!"

Mr. Hatchett points a finger at her. "No, sweetie. That's not true. I promised I would *try* to drive you." To me, he says, "Her mother had a crisis at the office this morning, had to get in early and I—"

Something chirps inside his suit jacket. "Oh, great," he says, whipping out his cordless. "Hatchett here," he says into the phone. "What?! No, no, no. The *Martins* file. I need copies of the *Martins* file. Yes, have it on my desk. Look, I'm catching the—"

He studies his watch. "I'm catching the seven thirty-one so I'll be in my office by eight forty-six."

He hangs up without saying good-bye. "Okay," he says, "so we're all set here and Freddy is going to watch out for you and—"

"But Daddy!" Sam cries.

He sighs. "Yes, sweetheart . . ."

She looks down, red-faced. She lowers her voice. "I'm *scared* of the bus."

"I know you are, sweetie, but that's just because you've never ridden it before. Everything's a little scary the first time. Right, Freddy?"

He grins at me. I nod back. I'm thinking. I'm going to flunk, I'm going to flunk, I'm going to—

"Look, Sam. We've been here for—what? Two weeks now? And Mommy or I has driven you to school every morning. Now we can't keep that up. You've just gotta get over this little hurdle. Okay? Okay. I gotta fly. Give me a smile."

She gives him a huge fake grin. He gives her shoulders a brief squeeze. Then, holding his suit jacket closed around him, he jogs up the street.

Sam and I are alone.

I force myself to smile. "Hi," I say.

Sam looks down at the street and kicks a pebble.

"Listen," I say, "I have this math take-home test I gotta work on. And the bus is going to be here any second. You don't mind if I . . . ?"

I reach for my backpack. Sam gives a snort of disgust, like she can't believe anyone could be so rude.

"Look, I'm sorry," I say, "but if I don't do this test, I'll flunk."

Sam rolls her eyes. Then she looks hurt. Her lower lip starts to tremble.

Oh, no. Don't cry. That's all I need.

I hop my skateboard onto the curb, then down again. I can tell Sam's watching.

I take this skateboard with me everywhere. They don't let you bring skateboards into our school. What I do is, I hide it under my coat and stash it in my locker.

I know what you're going to say. Skateboards aren't cool anymore. Now every kid is into Rollerblades. I guess that's just another thing I'm late about. All the trends.

"Want to ride?" I ask.

I'm such a nice guy, aren't I? Do me a favor. After I flunk out of school, tell my parents how nice I am.

Sam shakes her head. No, she doesn't want to ride. But at least she doesn't look like she's going to cry anymore.

I hear an engine rev. Mr. Hatchett backs his black Porsche out of his driveway so fast he almost knocks down his mailbox. He honks twice for good-bye as he peels out.

"Don't *you* have any homework?" I ask Sam.

"I finished it," she mutters.

"Oooh," I say, "Miss Smarty-pants."

That makes her smile, but only a little. "How old are you, anyway?" I ask.

She holds up her hand and wiggles all five fingers. "Fifty?"

She smiles a little more.

I hear the familiar wheeze of a big diesel engine. I look up as—

The big yellow school bus turns onto my street. It's only two blocks away.

"Hey! Here comes the bus!" I tell Sam.

I try to make my voice sound all cheery, like this is really great news for Sam. Hooray! The bus! Then I pick up my skateboard and hold out my hand to—

Uh-oh.

Sam opens and closes her fists as if she's getting ready for a fistfight. One tear leaks out of her eye and inches down her cheek. That kills me. I feel so sorry for her all of a sudden. Please don't feel sorry for her, Freddy. You don't have time to feel sorry for her. Feel sorry for yourself if you want to feel sorry for—

"Aw," I say, "don't be scared."

Sam breathes hard. Her chest goes in and out. She wipes away the tear with the back of her hand. She wipes it fast, like maybe I won't see it.

"Nothing bad is going to happen to you," I promise her. "Hey. It's just a school bus."

Another tear. Another.

"And I'm going to keep you company the whole way," I say.

What am I saying? There goes math. Welcome to F City.

"Besides," I tell Sam, "it's not like there are bad kids on the bus. Is that what scares you? Bullies? Because I give you my word. There are no bullies on the—"

You know what? From the look on Sam's face, I just made a big mistake. I shouldn't have brought up bullies.

Bullies are something that are kind of on my mind these days. There are these two kids in my class, Mike and Jay? Somehow they got the crazy notion in their heads that I'm a good kid to pick on and—

Yup. It was definitely a mistake to bring up bullies.

Sam is racing back up the street.

"Sam!" I call. "Stop! Where are you . . . ? Sam!"

I run after her. But she has too big a lead.

And as she runs *up* the street the school bus roars *down* the street. It's coming right at us.

Suddenly Sam darts right in front of the—

"SAM!" I scream.

CHAPTER 5

THE BUS HONKS AND SCREECHES ITS BRAKES. I HOLD
my skateboard in front of my face.

Not much of a hero, I know. But I can't watch.

The last thing I see is the big bus about to smack
Sam's little body into bits.

I keep the skateboard over my eyes. When I pull it
down, it's as if—

Time has stood still.

Nothing has changed. Sam stands in front of the
bus, staring up at it. I guess the bus braked just in
time.

I run over to Sam. Except just then she starts to
run again. I have to run and grab her.

"Hey!" I gasp. "Sam—C'mon. It's—Okay!"

She wriggles like crazy. The bus honks hard.
We're going to miss it! I don't know what to do.

So what I do is, I pick Sam up, hold her and the
skateboard together. She kicks and punches the air.

But I don't let go. I carry her around to the bus door as she flips and flops like a little fish.

"I'm not going!" she wails. "I'm not going!"

I can see old Dickerson scowling down at us from the driver's seat. I can see kids gaping out the windows.

I think about Mr. Hatchett. He made it seem like this was going to be so easy. Halloween is coming up, Mr. Hatchett. How'd you like a broken egg right on the old Porsche?

I put Sam back down and kneel in front of her. "So," I say, "I guess you *are* a little bit scared of the old bus. Ha-ha."

Sam doesn't laugh.

"You coming or not?" Mr. Dickerson growls.

Mr. Friendly. Mr. I-Love-Children.

Mr. Dickerson is this bony old guy with wrinkles and a big Adam's apple that goes up and down when he talks. I have trouble keeping my eyes off it.

"We're coming," I tell him.

Sam has her hands over her face. I make her take them down. "Look," I tell her, "I give you my word that nothing bad will happen to you on this bus. And when I give my word, I never go back on it. Never."

This isn't true. In fact, it's another thing my parents always get on my case about. How I never keep my word. But I figure right now isn't a good time to get into that with Sam.

"Okay?" I ask her.

She nods.

Yesss! Finally!

I take her hand. It's wet with sweat. Or maybe mine is. Then I turn to lead her onto the bus.

The bus is gone!

CHAPTER 6

WHILE SAM AND I WERE TALKING, MR. DICKERSON drove off down the street. Cute.

He has to turn around in front of my house. See, I live at the end of Cedar Lane, which is a dead end.

On his way back, Dickerson stops and lets us get on. I pop a wheelie to get my skateboard onto the first step, which always annoys Mr. Dickerson. Then, as I carry my skateboard onto the bus, I grin at him really hard.

"I have a schedule," he mutters, staring straight ahead.

He reaches down for the big metal lever that pulls the door shut and pulls in the big red stop sign on the other side of the bus. And . . . we're off.

Sam and I stare down the aisle. We see kids shouting, switching seats, playing tag, opening windows, shutting windows, springing up behind kids' seats and pulling their hair—

The usual.

But this morning, it's like I see the bus through Sam's eyes. She has a point. It does look kind of scary.

By the time the bus gets to my stop, it's about half-full. Most of the kids are middle-schoolers, like me. But there are one or two younger kids, like Sam. Sitting in the first seat are Betsy Gold and Anna Rivers, two sixth-graders from my class who are always giggling at me. They're kind of annoying, if you want to know the truth.

Right away they start chanting, "Freddy has a girlfriend, Freddy has a girlfriend."

I take a bow.

I high-five with a few kids as I lead Sam to an empty seat. I take off my backpack and toss it down. Then I put my skateboard wheels up on the floor. I sit by the window and Sam sits next to me.

"Well, that was easy," I say. I wipe my forehead with the sleeve of my denim jacket. "You're not planning any more tricks like that, are you? Like running in front of the bus? Because I have a ton of homework to do."

Sam makes a face like she's sniffing the air.

She's wearing this blue corduroy jacket. She still has her hood on. It's hot on the bus, especially after being outside in the cold. Smells bad in here, too, like kids' sweating and sour milk baking. I lean over and fumble with the laces on Sam's hood and take it off.

Underneath the hood she has black hair, which she wears in a ponytail. The ponytail sticks straight up from her head like a squirrel's tail. It's pretty cute, I have to admit.

I unzip her coat and help her off with her backpack. Then I see that Sam's nose is running. Green gooey snot. GROSS!

Mr. Hatchett? Make that eggs and soap on your Porsche for Halloween.

I scrounge around in my pocket till I find an old Tasty Freeze napkin. "Here," I say, handing Sam the napkin. "Would you wipe that, please? I think I'm gonna puke."

She won't take the napkin. Oh, come *on*! What? You're going to make *me* wipe your nose for you?

That's exactly what she's going to do. Sighing, I lean over. "Hold on," I say.

She turns her head away fast, but when I wipe her nose, she holds still. I sort of close my eyes while I do it. Then I ball up the napkin hard and stuff it deep into my jacket pocket.

Then we're silent again.

"Well," I say, "homework time."

"Why does that window say 'Emergency'?" Sam asks.

She's right. We're sitting next to one of the emergency windows. "It's an emergency window," I say quickly. I want to get off this topic as fast as possible.

"Why do we need an emergency window?" she asks. Her voice sounds hollow.

"For an emergency. Now if you don't mind . . ." I start to open my backpack.

"I want to get off," Sam says.

"Sam, the emergency-window thing is just in case, you know? Emergencies never happen. Anyway, it's good we're sitting here. Anything happens, open the window and bingo. We're out of here."

I open my backpack. Sam looks around. Now she spots the emergency *doors*. There are four of those. One on either side of the bus, one in the very very back, and one in the roof. It's the door in the roof that gets Sam's attention. "What's *that* door for?" she asks, pointing up.

I never thought about it. I guess if the bus is in some big pileup and tips over and is about to blow up or something, the roof will be the only way out. I sure don't want to get into *that*.

"They had an emergency door left over, so they stuck it up there," I say.

"I think I'm going to throw up," she says.

"Really?"

She starts rocking back and forth.

"Oh, no," I say. "Sam, come on. Don't do that."

She lurches at me.

Her mouth opens wide.

She's going to barf all over me!

"Sam! Sam! What do I do? I mean, to keep you from throwing up? Put your head down! No, put your head back! I don't remember which. Oh no! Oh no!"

Sam closes her eyes and breathes really hard. Then she opens her eyes again. She stares at me. "False alarm," she says. She looks a little green. But she gives me a tiny smile.

I breathe deep and slow, trying to get my heart rate back to normal.

Two heads pop up like jack-in-the-boxes above the seat.

"Hi," the heads say together.

Betsy and Anna. I fake a grin.

"So who's this?" Betsy asks me.

"This is Sam Hatchett," I say. "She's my new neighbor."

"Hi, Sam," Betsy and Anna say together. Betsy reaches over the seat to shake Sam's hand. Sam seems to like that.

"Freddy," Anna asks me, "can we talk to you in private for a second?"

"Why?"

" 'Cause we have something to talk about that"—
she nods her head at Sam—"she shouldn't hear."

"Just say it," I tell Anna.

"You tell," Anna says to Betsy.

"No you," Betsy answers.

"*Somebody* tell," I say.

Betsy has a round moon face. She goes out for all
the school plays. Right now she makes this face like
she has the most earth-shattering news of all time.
"Guess who's going to be on the bus today?" she asks
me. "You'll die when you hear. Guess. Guess who's
coming on the bus!"

"Barney," I say, "live."

"Mike and Jay," says Anna, snapping her gum.

I feel something flip over inside my stomach.
Great. Now *I'm* going to throw up.

"Oh, yeah, *right*," I say.

"I'm totally serious," says Betsy.

Sam's jaw drops. "Who's Mike and Jay?" she asks.

"Nobody," I tell her. "And they're not going to be
on the bus, so don't worry."

"Are they bullies?" Sam asks Anna.

Anna shakes her head at Sam, as if to say that
Mike and Jay are nothing to worry about. Oh, yeah.
Like that's going to fool her. Sam is five. She's not
dumb.

I can feel Sam looking at me. I know what she's
thinking. I said there wouldn't be any bullies on the
bus. And now—

"Mike and Jay live right near school," I tell Sam.
"They never take the bus. Never." I smile, but a drop
of sweat runs down my forehead.

It's true. Mike and Jay never take the bus. I don't
have to worry about them torturing me until recess.
So why are Betsy and Anna looking at each other
like they just found out I have some horrible disease
and they can't bear to tell me?

"*What?!*" I say.

"Mike and Jay slept over at their cousin Steve's house last night," Betsy whispers, making her voice all scary-scary. "That's way far from school. They *have* to take the bus."

It's not true, I tell myself. It's not true. But my heart beats faster.

"Where did you hear that?" I demand.

"From Steve's sister," Anna says. She snaps her gum.

Anna Rivers has dirty-blond hair, beady blue eyes, a bumpy nose, and a scrawny neck. She's always snapping her gum and making remarks. Sometimes I think Betsy wouldn't be so hard to take if she didn't hang out with Anna all the time. Now Anna snaps her gum again and adds, "Scout's honor."

"Scout's nothing," I say. "That's bull."

"I hope you're right," Betsy says, sounding scared.

"Listen," I say, "if you two don't mind. I've got a lot of homework to do and—"

I nod my head toward Sam, trying to show them why I need them to shut up.

Anna shrugs. "C'mon," she says, "let's leave these two lovebirds alone."

The girls laugh, then they disappear.

I look down at Sam. She's staring right at me.

"They won't be on the bus," I say.

She keeps staring.

"I promise."

But I can tell she doesn't believe me.

And a few minutes later . . .

Betsy and Anna pop up over our seat again. Their faces look white as paper.

"What?" I ask, feeling instantly pukey.

"Look out the window," Betsy tells me as the bus slows down. She keeps her voice low.

"Why?"

"Just do it."

Anna has her head near the window. "Oh no oh no," she mumbles.

I tell myself they're only teasing. Then I look. My heart races.

"See?" Betsy whispers. "And you said I was kidding. Now what are we going to do? *What?*"

"Who is it?" Sam asks, tugging on my sleeve. "Who is it?!"

Anna turns and gives Sam a big grin. "It's Mike and Jay."

CHAPTER 7

"**I**S IT?" SAM ASKS ME. "IS IT? IS IT? IS IT? IS IT?"

The thing is, I can't see past Anna. That makes me very nervous.

The bus stops.

The doors squeak open.

I hold my breath.

Nick Haggerty, a skinny seventh grader with terrible pimples, boards the bus. When he sees us he grins and waves. "Hey, good morning!" he calls in his singsong voice.

I sink back against the seat with a sigh.

"Burn!" Anna shrieks.

She and Betsy bounce up and down in their seats, laughing and clapping.

"Did you see how scared Freddy was?" Anna cries. "Did you see?"

"It was *my* idea," Betsy tells me shyly, like she's really proud of herself.

"What is wrong with you two?" I ask. "Seriously. Have you ever considered getting mental help?"

Both girls look surprised—then hurt. "We were just trying to be funny," Anna says.

I glance at Sam. She's rocking back and forth. If it wasn't for Sam, maybe I'd think it *was* funny.

"It's okay, Sam, don't worry," I say. "I told you they were making it up."

Sam rocks on. "It wasn't make up," she mutters, shaking her head. She says it over and over.

I look up at Betsy and Anna. They're watching Sam. They look worried. Well, it's a little late for that.

"Nice going," I snap at them.

"It was all made up, Sam," Anna says.

"Yeah," agrees Betsy, "all except the part about how they slept over at their cousin's house."

Anna nudges her hard.

"What?" Betsy says.

And now I'm feeling all nervous again. Was that part really true? Did they really sleep over at—

"C'mon," Anna tells Betsy, tugging her arm. The girls head back to their seats and leave us in peace. Finally.

"Morons," I grumble.

I look over at Sam. She clutches her lunch box and her bunny doll and stares straight ahead at the metal back of the seat ahead of us. There's all this graffiti scratched into the metal, plus wads of old gum. Not much of a view.

Just then, some kids in the back row start blasting out a round of "Great Big Gobs of Greasy Grimy Gopher Guts."

I look at my watch. Seven-thirty. Seven-thirty?!

Have you ever noticed that when you need time to go slow, it speeds up? I'm dying to start my homework, but how can I when Sam is like this? Thanks to Betsy and Anna, she looks more nervous than ever.

"Does that bunny rabbit have a name?" I ask.

No response.

"*Kickboxing Kangaroos,*" I say, studying her lunch box. "Is that a good show?"

No answer.

"Oh come on, Sam," I say, "would you lighten up?"

She gives me a quick glare, then goes back to staring straight ahead.

"What are you worrying about? Mike and Jay?"

She turns to face me. "I'm not worrying about Mike and Jay," she says. Then she goes back to staring at the seat.

"Good," I say. "Because there's no reason to be worried about them."

I open my notebook. But just then—

The bus slows down, making another stop. I glance out the window to see who we're picking up.

My mouth drops open.

I don't want to say anything. I don't want to scare Sam. But it's like the words just fall out of my mouth.

"Oh . . . NO!!!"

CHAPTER 8

STEVE GLEASON GETS ON THE BUS FIRST. RIGHT BEHIND
Steve comes—

Mike and Jay.

Mike and Jay don't look alike. Mike has a fat head
and a blond crew cut. He usually has this expression
on his face like he just plugged his thumb into the
electrical socket. Jay is tall for a twelve-year-old.
He's muscular and well built with flaming red hair
and freckles.

But to me, these two idiots look pretty much the
same. For one thing, they both always leave their
mouths hanging open, like a couple of dogs.

I glance at Sam. She clenches her jaw so hard her
head shakes. I guess she knows who it is without
having to ask. But then, she doesn't have to be a genius to figure *that* out.

Sam isn't the only one who's scared. The whole

bus grows quiet. I mean, kids are still talking and stuff, but nowhere near as loud as before.

Steve sits down quick. Not Mike and Jay.

"Good morning, suckers!" Mike shouts. Then he pulls up his sweater and shirt and slaps his big bare belly. Jay throws back his head and hollers like a wolf.

You would think Mr. Dickerson would say something. Like at least he could tell them to sit down. But Dickerson just closes the bus door and drives off.

Mike and Jay saunter down the aisle. Jay has one hand in the front pocket of his sweatshirt.

That worries me.

It's the kind of pocket that goes all the way across the sweatshirt. A big pocket. Big enough for a hunting knife.

On the first day of school this year, Jay got caught with a knife. He stabbed a kid during homeroom. Turned out it was a rubber knife, but Ms. Marville almost had a heart attack.

Jerks . . .

As Mike and Jay swagger down the aisle they slap a few kids' heads. Lunge at kids, too.

I keep my eyes right on them. I stare at that hand in Jay's pocket. He keeps his hand well hidden. That worries me even more.

I think bullies are like dogs. They smell fear.

Maybe if I wasn't scared, not even a little bit, Mike and Jay would leave me alone.

The only problem is, I'm very scared.

And they stop right at our seat.

CHAPTER 9

"**M**ORNING, BEAVERHEAD," MIKE SAYS. "LOOK, JAY, it's Beaverhead."

"Hi, Beaverhead!"

Every kid has something that really gets to him. Like their braces or their zits. With me, it's this Beaverhead business. See, my two front teeth are kind of big. And then I've got this brown hair that's short and coarse and looks a little like fur. So whenever anyone calls me Beaverhead, my stomach churns like a washing machine.

"Don't pay any attention," I tell Sam.

Oh, right. Like she can just ignore them. They're hanging all over our seat. Their heads bob and their bodies sway with the motion of the bus. Their mouths hang open. They grin at me.

"Hear that, Jay?" Mike asks. "Beaverhead says she shouldn't pay any attention."

"I heard," says Jay, his eyes boring into mine.

"Maybe you should show him what you brought to school today for show-and-tell?" suggests Mike. "Maybe that will get his attention."

"You want to see what I brought for show-and-tell, Beaverhead?" asks Jay.

I want to say no. In fact, I want to beg them not to show me or tell me. But I figure that wouldn't be too cool. Also I'm afraid to say anything, because I don't know if my voice will shake. So all I do is, I keep my eyes right on Jay's, like that will show him I'm not scared.

He glares back.

I can feel Sam's eyes on me, too. I know she expects me to do something.

Sure—but what?

"Wait till you see, Beaverhead," Jay tells me. "You're going to love it."

I have a feeling he's wrong about that.

He pulls his hand out of his pocket, pulls it out real slow.

I almost faint.

Jay's got a gun!

CHAPTER 10

THE GUN IS BLACK AND SHINY. IT LOOKS BIG ENOUGH TO blow my entire head off.

Jay smiles. "What do you say, Beaverhead?" He points the gun right at me.

I breathe hard and fast. I don't know about you, but I've never had a gun pointed at me. And now that I'm having that experience, I don't want to have it ever again. It's horrible. It's worse than horrible. It's—

"Put that away," I say. "Now."

Oh, great idea. Like I can just give Jay Hefferton an order and he'll say, "Sure." And do whatever I say.

Surprise, surprise. It doesn't work. For one thing, my mouth has gone dry and my voice cracks, so you can barely understand what I'm saying.

And Jay, he just grins like he's posing for a picture.

"I said put it away," I repeat, but now it sounds like I'm begging.

"Put it away," Mike mimics in a baby voice.

They won't shoot me. No way! They're just trying to scare me. Well, it's working. Working like a charm. I can't breathe.

Just then Anna comes running down the aisle. She plops down in the seat right across from us.

Wow. I've never been so glad to see Anna before, let me tell you. Then again, I've never been glad to see her at all, so it isn't much of a contest.

Anna waves for Betsy to come, too. Betsy starts down the aisle, but stops again, looking petrified. Join the club.

"What's going on?" Anna asks, pretending she doesn't know.

"Beat it," Mike tells her.

Anna doesn't beat it. Instead she stands up and yells, "Mr. Dickerson! Jay Hefferton has a gun!"

"Shut up or you die next," Jay snarls at her.

"Oh, like I'm really scared," Anna says.

I'm stunned. Anna is being so brave. Maybe Anna isn't so bad after all.

"What's your name, little twerp?" Mike asks Sam.

Sam looks at me, like she wants to know what she's supposed to do.

And you know what? More than ever I'm wishing I didn't have to look after her on this trip. Because if I was alone right now, I could use some of my usual methods for dealing with bullies. Like falling to the ground and begging. Or screaming and crying for the bus driver to help me. But I don't feel like I can do that with Sam here. Especially after I said I'd look after her!

"What's the matter, kid?" Jay asks Sam, sneering. "You don't know your own name?"

"It's Sam," Sam says, rolling her eyes.

Look at her. Five years old and she's acting braver than I am.

"Sam?!" Mike says. *"Sam???"* He and Jay both guffaw.

"It's short for Samantha!" Sam says, looking hurt.

Well, that's one good thing. I'm about to get shot to death, but at least I guessed right about Sam's name.

"Sam," Jay says again, still laughing. "What a name for a girl!"

This is worse than when they were picking on me. Picking on Sam—it really makes me mad.

"Hey!" I tell Jay. "Get lost, freckle-dork." My voice gets loud, too. No more cracking.

Jay stares at me, his mouth hanging open. "What did you call me?"

I want to lie and change what I said. It didn't sound like a very good insult the first time I said it. But that was what came out of my mouth and now I'm stuck with it.

"Freckle-dork," I repeat. I try to make it sound like the greatest insult ever invented.

"Hey!" Jay suddenly raises his voice. "I've got a gun here, Beaverhead. Do you see that?"

"I see that."

"So shut up!"

"You shut up," I say.

This whole brave thing—once you start, it's not so easy to stop. I can't believe I'm saying these things. I really can't. Maybe it's because Anna and Sam are acting so tough, and that's making me want to act tough, too.

I stare at the tiny hole at the end of Jay's gun, waiting for him to fire. Okay, I think. I'm going to die.

Then I think of something else.

Something that makes me feel a whole lot braver.

But before I can do anything about this new thing that I'm thinking, Sam bolts out of her seat.

She doesn't get far. Mike holds her back.

Suddenly I lean over and karate-chop Jay's hand as hard as I can. The hand that's holding the gun.

In the movies, this would work perfectly. Jay would scream and drop the gun.

But the thing is, I don't know karate. So all that happens is Jay looks surprised. Then he whacks me with the back of his hand, right in the shoulder. He's wearing a watch, too, so it hurts extra.

Then Jay turns the gun on Sam.

"Cut it out!" I yell, diving at the gun and pushing it away. "What's the matter with you?"

Jay pulls the gun away from me. I try to grab his arm, but he yanks it free. He shoves me. So does Mike. And then—

Jay is no dummy. He knows what will really get me.

'Cause he doesn't shoot me.

He shoots Sam. Right in the chest.

CHAPTER 11

SOME OF THE WATER BOUNCES OFF SAM'S METAL LUNCH box. But some of the water squirts her coat.

I'm out of my seat like a shot. I punch Jay. He drops the gun on the floor. I start screaming.

I've never punched anyone in my life.

I once asked Dad what I should do if I had to fight somebody. He said, "Talk your way out of it."

"But what if I can't talk my way out of it?" I asked him.

He said, "Run."

I'm not kidding. Those were his exact words.

So no one's ever taught me anything about fighting.

Well, I think I just learned something. I think I just learned a very important lesson.

It's a bad idea to make a fist with your thumb inside your other fingers. Because you break your thumb. At least, that's what it feels like I just did.

Anyway, I'm screaming louder than Jay.

And it's two against one. And they're standing and I'm half sitting. And they pull me past Sam. And—

This is strange. I was sitting just a second ago. Now I'm lying down in the aisle and—

They're hitting me. You're not supposed to hit a kid when he's down, right?

Who should I explain that to?

I hear kids screaming. I twist this way and that, but I can't get away. Mike and Jay have me sandwiched.

And then I see Mike smile as he pulls his foot back. It's a big work boot, too.

I try to roll away.

But I roll right into Jay.

He's got his foot pulled way back, too. He's going to kick me right in the stomach!

CHAPTER 12

"**S**TOP RIGHT NOW!" ROARS MR. DICKERSON.

The foot that's about to kick me stops in midair.

"I SAID STOP!"

Mike and Jay look up. Not like they're scared. More like they're curious what Dickerson has to say.

I raise my head. Dickerson stands at the head of the aisle, red in the face.

Hey. Shouldn't he be driving the bus?

I feel a moment of panic until I realize—of course—he parked the bus by the side of the road.

"OFF THE BUS!" Dickerson shouts. "ALL THREE OF YOU!"

Mike and Jay wait until he screams it a few more times, just to show they don't have to listen to him if they don't want to. Then they stroll down the aisle. Like they've been invited to a birthday party at Dickerson's house.

"You, too!" Dickerson yells at me.

I just lie here.

"I said you, too!"

I can't believe this. After all the times Mike and Jay hit me, I need an ambulance and a stretcher. Instead Dickerson is kicking me off the bus. "They attacked me!" I yell up at the roof of the bus.

"I don't care who started it," Dickerson yells right back. "Off!"

Wouldn't you know. I finally catch the stupid bus, then I get thrown off it.

I'm beginning to think this whole day is—

"Hurry it up!" Dickerson yells. He really is crazy angry.

I get up. And as I get up I realize something. Something good. I feel proud of myself. I mean, I know I lost the fight, but I was the one who started it. That has to count for something.

"OFF!" shouts Dickerson.

"I'm going," I mutter.

I'm about to walk down the aisle and get off the bus when I see Sam looking up at me.

And then—

I realize something else. Something that feels like it's going to blow the top of my head right off.

I stare down the aisle at Dickerson. I have to look past a sea of kids' faces. Everyone is turned around in their seats, watching me.

"I can't go," I say.

I'm breathing hard. And for some reason I have this giant lump in my throat.

Mr. Dickerson doesn't say anything. But he looks madder than I've ever seen him. "What did you say?"

"I said . . . I can't go."

And I can't. Because I promised Sam I'd protect her. I can't protect her very well if I get thrown off the bus, now can I? And, see . . .

I've broken a lot of promises in my life. In fact I've broken just about every promise I ever made.

But I just decided this is one promise I'm going to keep.

No matter what.

CHAPTER 13

DICKERSON'S ADAM'S APPLE BOBS UP AND DOWN LIKE it's about to explode. He points a bony finger at the bus door.

"Off!"

I shake my head. Nope. Not going, I tell myself.

"Not going," I tell him.

There's other stuff I could tell him. Mr. Hatchett—Sam's own dad—ditched her this morning. I'm not going to ditch her, too. I mean, she was scared to begin with. Now she's got to be feeling really really scared, after Mike and Jay.

Mr. Dickerson glares at me, like he's trying to think of a punishment horrible enough for my crime. "I'll deal with you in a minute," he snarls. Then he turns and stomps off the bus.

All at once the bus goes nuts with shouting and cheering. It's hard to hear everything the kids yell, but I can tell they admire me for standing up to Mike and Jay and Mr. Dickerson, too.

Then every kid sitting on the left side of the bus rushes to the windows on the right side of the bus. It's amazing the whole bus doesn't tip over. Everyone wants to watch Mr. Dickerson chew out Mike and Jay. Or watch him try.

"You okay?"

I turn. Anna looks up at me with worried little blue eyes. She snaps her gum.

"Me? I'm fine," I say. I clap. "And the best thing is, I figure now I can get out of gym for sure. Ow." I hug myself.

Anna laughs. I laugh, too.

Sam tugs on my sleeve. She doesn't say anything. She just beams at me.

"I wasn't scared," she says.

I grin and tug lightly on her ponytail.

"I knew it was a water pistol," she adds.

"Me, too," I say.

Which is sort of true. See, that was what I realized right before I got real brave and tried my karate chop. I realized that no gun had bullets that teensy-weensy. Once I saw the tiny hole at the end of Jay's gun, I was home free.

I look out the window. I can see Mr. Dickerson talking to Mike and Jay. The way he's waving his hands in the air, he doesn't look like he's really letting them have it, though. It's more like he's begging them to behave themselves.

We're parked on Main Street in downtown Elmsford. Elmsford is a quiet place. Tiny, too. The whole downtown is only three blocks long. There's a post office, a grocery, a hardware store, a barbershop, a stationery store, a toy store, and a bank. We're parked right outside the bank.

I smile down at Sam, trying to make sure she feels okay.

"See," I say. "Riding a bus isn't so scary."

She giggles. "You were great," she says.

"I was?"

"You stood up to them."

"I was on the floor, Sam."

"You were awesome," she insists. She looks so grateful, I promise myself all over again . . .

I'm sticking with Sam.

"Yeah, you were great," Anna agrees.

Not a bad day after all. Maybe I can get thrown down on the floor a few more times, and I'll really be a hero.

"Hey," says Sam. She frowns down at her watch. "It's getting late . . . your homework!"

"Ah, don't worry about that," I say.

Hey. Whatever Mr. Himmelfarb will do to me, I figure he won't hit me like Mike and Jay did. So who cares?

Outside, Mike and Jay beg Dickerson to let them back on the bus. They're practically crying. But that's just a trick they pull whenever they get in big trouble. There's no way Dickerson will be stupid enough to fall for that old crying trick. Is there?

And then—

I hear what sounds like a gigantic alarm clock going off.

Or a really loud phone that's off the hook.

I don't think much about it.

Until I see the men coming out of the bank.

THERE ARE TWO OF THEM. BOTH WEAR BLACK SKI
masks. In fact, they look identical.

Both men are tall and thin. Both men carry a
large black garbage bag, like the kind Dad uses
when he rakes the leaves. But that's not the main
thing. Down low by their sides, both men carry
guns.

Real ones.

I stare at those guns like I'm hypnotized. Seriously. It's like my eyes leave the bus and zoom out
the window and sit right on top of those weapons.

Guns!

The men walk fast. But they don't run. Just stride
through the cool fall air and the bright sunshine.
They look so strange and scary in their masks. But
all around them everything looks like it always did.
Good old downtown Elmsford.

Half a block away, a woman strolls with a baby in

a baby carrier hung from her chest. Right outside the bus, Mr. Dickerson goes on chewing out Mike and Jay. He looks up at the bank once or twice, I guess because of the alarm. But that's it.

And since the driver is off the bus, the kids *on* the bus roughhouse like mad. I think I'm one of the only ones who even notices.

The men in the masks toss their garbage bags in the backseat of a beat-up beige Ford Taurus that's parked right ahead of the bus. Then they get in the front seat.

They don't drive off, though. They just sit there.

If that's the getaway car, why doesn't it get away? I think.

I'm not thinking very much, though. It's like my whole life has gone into super slo mo.

I hear the whine of a car motor. Sounds like it won't turn over. And then my brain tells me the answer to my question. The men can't leave because their car won't start.

"What are you looking at?" Sam asks me.

I don't answer. I just keep staring down the aisle and out the windshield of the bus as—

The doors of the Taurus open and the two men get out again. Still wearing masks. Still carrying guns.

I have to tell you something. I haven't been in too many emergencies. But I've been in enough to know how I react. Which is to say, I have no reaction whatsoever.

One time I was at Alan Davis's house hanging out by the pool? This baby fell right in. I was not one of the kids who dove into the water and saved the baby. I was one of the kids who just stood there and watched like a fool.

Or take burglars. Lots of nights I wake up and listen to the sounds in the house and I'm sure I hear a prowler. So what do I do? I lie very still and hope I faint myself back to sleep.

But I shouldn't be thinking about this now. Because I'm doing it again. I'm freezing up. Standing here thinking about the past when I should be—

C'mon, Freddy! Don't stop now! You just got beat up by Mike and Jay. You're on a roll!

I climb past Sam and dive at the window. I pull the metal release levers and yank the window down so I can warn Mr. Dickerson.

Oops.

I forgot it was the emergency window. The whole pane of glass falls out and shatters on the sidewalk.

That sure gets Mr. Dickerson's attention. He whirls around and starts shrieking.

"Go!" I yell at him. Except I can't get any wetness in my mouth and barely any sound comes out.

It would take a lot of sound to get Dickerson to hear me, the way he's yelling.

I look out the front of the bus. The bank robbers stand outside their car. They turn their heads this way and that, like they have no idea what to do next.

Then one of the robbers turns—

And stares right at me.

CHAPTER 15

THE ROBBER ISN'T REALLY LOOKING AT ME. HE'S looking at the bus. I can tell what he's thinking, too. It's like he has a cartoon bubble over his head that says, "Bus!"

Then he turns to the other robber and says something. He points at the bus.

The other robber is jumping up and down like he has to go to the bathroom bad. But when he turns and sees the bus, he seems to calm down.

"What's going on?" Sam asks in a high voice.

I don't answer. I climb over Sam and into the aisle. Except I trip on my skateboard and go flying.

So I end up in Anna's lap.

"Hey there," she says, smiling.

I push away from her, trying to get my balance. I end up shoving her in the shoulder and the neck and the arm—like I'm pawing her.

She looks pretty shocked. I feel shocked, too, right in the middle of everything, that I touched her.

Anna giggles. I guess she doesn't know what's going on. I don't have time to tell her.

I race up the aisle.

I get to the front of the bus just as one of the robbers steps onto the first step.

Seeing the masked man coming toward me through that open door—

It's like seeing a monster come to life.

I grab the large round handle that works the door. I pull with all my might.

I close the door, too.

I shut the robber off the bus!

All except for his arm.

The arm with the gun.

Which is pointed right at me.

CHAPTER 16

HAVING A GUN POINTED AT ME—

It isn't like with Jay and Mike and their water pistol. This is like I could have a heart attack at any second and just die from being so terrified.

Maybe I did die. Maybe I'm dead.

No, I hear my heart. It's beating so fast I think it's going to blast out my mouth.

I start to open the door. The robber shoves it open the rest of the way. He races onto the bus. The other robber is right behind him.

The robbers are in such a rush they crash right into me. We go down in a heap.

Well, I'm on the floor again.

The two robbers shove each other as they struggle back to their feet. They're yelling at each other, too. Shouting things like, "Idiot!" and "Imbecile!" and "Get out of my way!"

Lying next to my head is—

Oh, wow. It's a wad of crisp, new $100 bills. The money is right next to my nose. It's got a dark smell, almost like mildew.

One of the robbers grabs the money and shoves it back in his garbage bag. He stashes the bag under the steering wheel and sits in the driver's seat. Then he pulls out fast. A lot faster than Mr. Dickerson ever drives, that's for sure.

The other robber says, "Here!" and gives the driver his trash bag. Then he stands in the aisle, peering out the window as we drive away. He's the nervous one. He's bouncing up and down again and saying, "Go, go, go, go!"

I get up. Kind of. I don't get up all the way. My legs feel so rubbery. I push my way back into a seat.

I sit right on top of somebody. I look around. I see a girl with a round face. I almost don't recognize her. She's so scared that her face looks totally different. Betsy. She doesn't say a word about the fact that I'm sitting on her. It's like she turned into a chair.

I move off her lap to the edge of the seat and look out the back window as we drive away. I can see Mr. Dickerson run into the street, waving at us. I can see Mike and Jay watching us go. Their mouths hang *way* open. Bye-bye, Mr. Dickerson. Bye-bye, Mike and Jay.

They disappear from sight.

The alarm from the bank gets smaller, too, until it's no louder than the whine of a mosquito.

And then all at once, it seems like every kid on the bus is screaming. Like it just occurred to them what's going on.

It *is* pretty hard to believe. The switch happened so fast. We got rid of Mike and Jay. We even got rid of Mr. Dickerson. But in their place we got—

The screams grow louder.

Our bus is pretty rowdy and noisy, like I've said.

But I've never heard screeching like *this*.

The robber in the aisle yells for quiet. But it doesn't do any good. He clutches his head, like the noise is going to kill him.

"Stop it!" he shouts.

But everyone keeps screaming.

So he points his gun . . .

And fires.

CHAPTER 17

BANG!

I can't breathe.

The robber just fired his gun.

That means, he killed somebody.

I turn to look and see who got shot.

I expect to see some kid lying in the aisle with blood all over him, his eyes staring straight up.

Instead, I see every kid on the bus staring back at me with the same zombie face I must be wearing. Then I see him. The robber. He pointed his gun straight up.

He's looking up where the bullet went. I look up, too. Up at the roof.

There's that emergency exit door that Sam was so worried about. Only now it has a tiny hole in it.

And right then I hear something that I've never heard in all the years I've been riding Elmsford School Bus #109.

I hear total and utter silence.

I don't mean the way things got quiet when Mike and Jay got on the bus. This is like—no sound. Nothing. Nobody moves either.

"See that?" the driver calls back. "And they say kids aren't well behaved anymore." He chuckles.

The robber who fired his gun starts moving around like crazy. He shifts his weight from one foot to the other, paces back and forth, like one of those tigers you see at the zoo who's gone crazy from too many years in a cage. I can see his eyes through the holes in his ski mask. Pale blue and filled with terror.

Well, that's a surprise. It never occurred to me that a robber could get scared, too. A lot of good that does me.

"George!" the robber calls to the driver. "My gun went off! My gun went off, George!"

"Yeah, I heard it," the driver says.

"But I didn't even mean to fire it, George!"

"Well, that's why you have to calm down," the driver says. And stop using my name, moron."

"What? Oh, yeah, sorry, sorry."

"I mean, you don't want me calling you Frank, do you? Huh, Frank? Do you, *Frank*?"

"No, no, you're right, George," says Frank. "And I said I was sorry!"

George slaps the wheel. "So stupid! A getaway car that won't start! Didn't I tell you to steal a new car? Didn't I tell you that?"

"Lay off, wouldya," Frank says, his voice shaking. "It wasn't easy stealing that car. I mean, you're the robber, not me."

"Oh, great," George says. "Tell my history to every kid on the bus, why don't you?! AND STOP CALLING ME GEORGE!"

"Sorry," Frank says. "Sorry, George. I mean, whatever."

Frank's hand shakes. Which means, the gun shakes. And sometimes, as Frank paces around, the gun shakes right at *me*.

"Just tell me this is all going to be okay," Frank pleads, pacing faster. "I mean, don't you think people are going to notice when a whole school bus is missing?"

"Don't worry," says George. "We just have to get to Washington Street."

Washington Street?

Washington Street?

I never even heard of Washington Street.

Where are they taking us? On a field trip to the White House?

Someone, I realize, is clutching my arm, and has been clutching it for a while. It's Betsy. She's shaking like a hummingbird.

And then—all at once—my whole body goes weak.

I just remembered who else is on the bus.

Someone I'm supposed to protect. Someone I told the bus was safe. Someone I promised . . .

I turn my head to look for Sam, but I can't see her.

"Oh, George!" Frank moans, swinging the gun through the air. Three rows of kids duck out of sight.

"Why did I let you talk me into this?" Frank cries. "Why, George, why? I'm not a robber. I'm a writer. No, I'm not a writer, I'm an actor. No, I'm a total mess-up, that's what I am. My mother is right. Everything I touch turns to garbage."

"Hey!" George yells at him. "Get a grip. We're going to be fine. Just hang in there for twenty more minutes and then we'll be—"

There's a sudden commotion. I turn. Anna is

standing up. She's trying to open a window. I guess she's going to yell for help.

Frank shouts, "Hey! You! Get down!"

She disappears from sight.

I can't believe how brave she's being. I just can't believe it. I don't think that I could ever—

I say a silent prayer. I pray that we get out of this terrible situation fast. Before—

Before I'm expected to be brave like Anna.

And then the next second—

Now I really can't believe it—

I'm doing something brave. Or maybe it's extremely stupid, I don't know. What I do is, I raise my hand. Like I'm in school.

"What?" Frank cries. He's pointing the gun right at me. Not on purpose. But so what?

Well, Freddy, you raised your hand. And the robber called on you. Now you better talk or he's going to get so frustrated that he'll—

"*What?!*" Frank yells, jumping up and down.

"Uh . . . sir . . . I was just wondering if . . . maybe you could just . . . let us off the bus, sir. We don't want . . . any trouble. Just . . . you know . . . let us off. Then we'll be out of your way."

Frank laughs hysterically. Then he stops laughing. "Hey, George? I think this kid has a good suggestion. He says we should—"

"Shut up," George says.

I look up. Through the little holes in his mask, I can see George's green eyes in the rearview mirror. George's eyes aren't filled with terror. They look calm. And angry.

"You shut up, too," George tells me.

I shut up.

"Don't be smart," he adds.

I tell myself to be very stupid.

"Because we got enough to worry about right now, you understand?"

I gulp.

George keeps his eyes locked on mine for another second. Just to make sure we understand each other.

Why did I have to raise my hand? Why?

Then George looks away. He raises his voice. "Okay, kiddies, listen up! As you can see, we had to borrow your bus for a little while. I'm sorry about that, but if you follow my instructions very carefully, no one's going to get hurt."

Someone starts sobbing. George waits for quiet. He gets it, too.

You know what just occurred to me?

I almost missed this bus.

The one day I *catch* the bus, look what happens.

"All you have to do," George says, "is keep your heads down and out of sight and keep your hands over your eyes. We're just going to take a little ride and then we'll be saying good-bye. You'll be a little late for school today, kiddies, but that's about it."

Late for school. Ten minutes ago I would have been very upset to hear that I was going to be late. Now—

"Now, if anyone has a problem with these rules," continues George, "just let us know, so we can blow your head off. Okay?"

All this time I'm still sitting with Betsy in the front seat. I keep turning my head, looking for Sam, and wondering if I can make it back to where she's sitting without getting my head blown off. Do I have the courage to try?

I'm pretty sure I don't.

Anyway, Anna is back there with her.

That's good enough, right? Right?

Oh, why did Mr. Hatchett put Sam on the bus? Why did Mr. Hatchett put Sam on the bus? Why did Mr. Hatchett—

Oh no. There's Sam. She's back down the aisle a ways, sitting in our old seat. Only she's getting up. She's carrying her backpack and lunch box, too. Oh, good thinking, Sam. Like the robbers are going to stop and give us all a lunch break.

Sam stares right at me. She takes a step up the aisle.

What are you doing, Sam? Don't come up here. Don't come up here!

I get halfway out of my seat. I shake my head. Hard.

Sam looks at me. Then at Frank.

And then—

She runs up the aisle to where I'm sitting.

Except Frank stands in her way. She stops right in front of him. He stares down at her. Then he yells, "George!"

I glance up at the driver. I can see those angry eyes lock on mine again.

"She wants to sit with me," I blurt out to the driver. "She's, uh, she's my sister, sir. She's scared. Please. Don't hurt us. Please!"

The driver's eyes burn into mine. I can feel the message he's sending me. He already warned me once not to cause trouble. Now here I go again.

Slowly, I stand up. I hold my hands out, palm up, to show I'm not going to try anything. Like what would I try?

"Please, we'll go right back to our seats and put our heads down just like you said."

"Stay where you are!" George yells.

I stay.

"Make her go back to her seat," George tells Frank.

"Right," Frank says. He looks at Sam. Then he screams, "GO!"

But Sam just stands there frozen and wide-eyed like she's never going to move again.

"George?" Frank calls.

"Okay, kiddies," George calls out, "we've got a little girl up here who has some trouble following instructions. So she's going to teach us all a lesson."

"Please," I say, "sir?"

"Hey!" George shouts at me. "I already told you to be quiet. Don't make me tell you again!"

I want to be quiet. I want that more than anybody. But I can't. "I—I'm s-sorry, but please," I stammer, "please, we don't want—any trouble, we just—"

"Now, what I'm going to do, little girl," George calls out, drowning me out. "What I'm going to do is I'm going to count to three. You have until three to run back to your little seat. Understand?"

Sam doesn't say a word. She doesn't even nod. She just stares at Frank, who keeps hissing at her and waving his hands like she's some wild animal he's trying to scare off.

"One!" calls George.

Sam doesn't move.

C'mon, Sam! Go!

"Go!" I yell at her, my voice all hoarse and strange. "Run! Now! Back to your seat! What are you waiting for? Go!"

But Sam doesn't go.

"Two!" yells George.

"Go!" I yell again, even louder, and now I'm waving my hands in the air, just like Frank. "Run! Run!"

I'm not the only one yelling. Anna inches up the aisle, shouting at Sam to come back. And some other kids who are sitting near Sam reach for her, trying to pull her backward. And—

Seems like everyone on the bus is yelling at Sam.

She turns her head slightly. Her big eyes stare at me through her thick glasses, begging me to help her.

George yells, "Three!"

CHAPTER 18

Everyone stops yelling. It's like time is standing still again. Like when Sam ran in front of the bus. Everyone sits as still as a statue, waiting to see what will happen next.

Sam doesn't move.

"Okay," George grumbles. "We gave her every warning. Go ahead, Frank. You know what to do."

Frank is going to shoot her! Frank is going to shoot her!

I brace myself. Because what I've decided is, I'm going to dive into Frank and knock his gun away. That's what I've decided.

Any second now, I'm going to do it.

The only thing is, I feel like someone took out all my bones. There's no way I can move.

But just then—

What's that sound?

Sure sounds like a siren.

In the distance.

Yes, definitely a siren.

Frank hears it, too. He looks up.

"George!" he cries.

"I heard it," George says.

Frank runs down the aisle and peers out the back window of the bus. "George!"

"Heads down!" George yells at us.

Every head drops out of sight.

I get my body moving again. "C'mon," I tell Sam, taking her hand. I drag her back down the aisle to the first empty seat, about four rows back from the driver.

It's a row with an emergency door. I push her over by the window side and scoot in after her.

"What do you think you're doing?" I whisper angrily. "Why would you run up to the front of the bus like that when there's a guy with a gun? Don't you have any sense?"

Nice. It's bad enough the bus is being hijacked. I have to yell at her.

"You said you would sit with me," Sam whispers back. She looks so pale I'm worried she's going to faint.

"I *was* sitting with you," I point out. "But something came up, in case you didn't notice."

"Heads down!" George yells at us.

We both put our heads down.

"I'm scared," Sam says.

"Well I'm scared, too."

"You said the bus was safe."

"Well, Sam, it's not like I lied. You think I knew there were going to be robbers on the bus? Give me a break."

It's weird. Arguing with Sam is helping to calm me down. It's a good thing Mr. Hatchett put Sam on the bus today, so she could look after me.

"I'm scared," she says again. Her voice is tiny, like a moan. And right away I feel so sorry for her all over again. Poor little kid.

"I want my rabbit," she whimpers.

"Your *what*?"

"My rabbit!"

"Oh, yeah. Your rabbit. Where is it?"

"I must have left it on the seat."

I was too scared to go down the aisle for *Sam*. There's no way I'm going back there for some rabbit.

"Forget the rabbit," I whisper. "Listen, it's going to be okay. Just stay quiet and keep your head down like he said and whatever you do, *don't move*."

I feel calm when I'm telling Sam to be calm. But then when I stop talking, I don't feel so calm anymore.

Because we're driving fast, faster than I've ever driven in a school bus. Or in anything for that matter.

But no matter how fast we go, that siren wails in the distance. Not getting louder. But not getting softer either.

"It's not going to be okay," Sam says. "It's not."

"Oh, sure," I say, "look on the bright side."

"You're an idiot," she says.

That takes me by surprise. I snort. I think that's so funny.

"Shut up over there," George calls.

"Sorry," I call back.

"I said shut up!"

I try to tell myself that this is like detention. Really really really bad detention. Only instead of getting more detention, if we mess up in here we get dead.

I hear George slapping the wheel. "Frank," he calls. "That kid is really starting to get on my nerves."

Frank hunches over in the back of the bus, watching out the back window. "Really?" he calls back to the driver. "That's what's getting on your nerves? That kid? What about that siren, George? That doesn't bother you? Or how about the fact that the siren is getting louder, George. It's getting louder!"

"Listen, Sam," I say in a tinier whisper. I put my hand on her knee. "No matter what happens, I'm going to stay right with you. Okay?" I squeeze her knee.

I'm crying. Just like that.

So weird. I comfort her and *I* start crying. But it's like, all of a sudden, I realize how much I wish there was someone saying this to *me*. Saying how they'll stick by *me* no matter what. Mom and Dad are always off working, ditching me just like Mr. Hatchett ditched Sam.

Get a grip, Freddy! I yell at myself. But I keep crying.

Sam doesn't look at me, but she nods. "Thank you, Freddy," she says, talking down at the floor.

Her saying thank you, somehow that makes me feel better. And now a good thing happens. The police siren gets even louder.

"George," Frank yells, thundering down the aisle to the driver's seat. "Please! I'm begging you! Go faster!"

Faster than this? I don't think the bus can go any—

Nope. The bus *can* go faster than this.

Sam keeps her head down. Good girl, Sam. But I don't follow the rules myself. I glance out the window.

Wowza. We are tearing—and I mean tearing—down Macklin Avenue.

And then Frank says, "Hey, George, didn't we just pass the turnoff to Morton Street?"

And right away there's the loudest—
SCREECH!!!

As George jams on the brakes we all rock forward, back.

"*Now* you tell me," George growls.

And just then, while the bus is stopped for an instant, something goes CLICK on the seat behind me.

It's a metal click.

Huh?

I turn fast, just as—

Sam opens the emergency door.

And starts climbing out.

CHAPTER 19

"**N**O, SAM!" I CRY. "WHAT ARE YOU—"

She gets one foot out the door as the bus backs up hard and fast. George is pulling a U-turn. Our tires spin as the bus drives off again. Fast.

I pull Sam back into the bus. "What are you doing?" I yell at her.

"You said! In an emergency!"

"When the bus is stopped!" I cry.

"Shut up back there!" yells George.

"It *was* stopped!" Sam insists, talking in this fierce whisper. She looks close to tears. I know I shouldn't yell at her. It's not going to calm her down any. But I can't help it. Here I'm trying so hard to protect her. Well, she's not making my job any easier.

"It stopped for one second!" I say, feeling my face turn red.

Oh no. The kids across from us must have spotted

the open emergency door because they're screaming at us, and pointing, too.

Frank runs over to our row. When he sees the open door, he stops cold.

"What are you doing?!" he shrieks. "George? It's that kid again! He's trying to climb off the bus!"

"Let him go!" George shouts back.

"Let him *go*?!"

"If he goes off the bus at this speed, he'll die," George explains. "Tell him to be my guest."

Nice guy. Mr. Always-With-The-Friendly-Suggestions.

"C'mon, I need you up here, Frank," George yells. "*Now*. I need directions."

"You're *lost*?" Frank wails, clutching his head.

"Just tell me where to go, wouldya?"

All this time the siren in the distance drones on. It's growing louder, louder.

Frank takes one more look at us, then charges back up front to the driver.

Sam tries to close the emergency door, but she can't. So the door swings open and flaps shut with a BANG! BANG! BANG!

Icy air whistles through the open door and cuts my face.

I try to reach over Sam and shut the door. But it swings away from me like it's teasing.

I lean out a little farther, grabbing at the handle.

Missed. And oh wow—What an awful sight.

The pavement blasts by underneath me.

I sit back. I have to close my eyes for a second.

"Sam, listen to me," I tell her. "Move away from that door till I can get it—"

I slap my hand at the door handle. I miss again.

"I'm—sorry," Sam says. "I messed up, didn't I?"

"No," I tell her. "It was a good idea. Really. I mean it."

I do mean it. It *was* a good idea. Maybe if I hadn't held her back, she could have made it out the emergency door. But that doesn't matter now because—

"That doesn't matter now!" I tell her. "Just move away from the door!"

"I thought—" Sam starts to say.

"I know! Just—Sam! Move!"

Sam starts to move away from the open door.

She does.

But just then George turns right so sharply that— Sam goes flying out the door.

CHAPTER 20

I SLAM MY HAND DOWN ON HER BACK AS SHE FALLS. I grab a handful of corduroy jacket. I hold on as tight as I can.

But—

Wait a minute. . . .

I unzipped this jacket, right?

And I untied the hood. . . .

And—

It's like I'm helping Sam off with her coat. The jacket comes right off in my hands!

"NO!" I cry. "NO!"

Sam falls.

CHAPTER 21

I GRAB ONE OF SAM'S WRISTS. SHE DANGLES OUT OF THE bus, screaming and crying.

I see gray pavement rocketing by. I see Sam's sneakers, dangling only inches from the street.

I reach down and try to grab her around the middle.

I'm leaning far out of the bus. We're both going to fall and die!

I lean farther out, trying to get a grip on her belt.

The wind rips me apart. Gum, pens, an old gym excuse, lunch money, and a decoder ring I got out of a cereal box all fly out of my pockets. I'm shouting.

Sam's foot almost bumps the pavement. If her sneaker touches that road, I know what will happen. Her foot will bend back. It will snap like a twig. Groaning, I lift her a couple of inches higher.

Then I feel her hand start to slip through mine.

CHAPTER 22

"**H**ANG ON!" I SHRIEK AT HER. "HANG ON!"

Back inside the bus, kids scream at the robbers, "STOP THE BUS! STOP THE BUS!"

Frank screams, too. But George screams at everyone that there's no way he's going to stop.

Just then I hear that cop car. It finally caught up with us. Too late, too late!

"PULL OVER TO THE SIDE OF THE ROAD," the cops bark over their microphone. "PULL OVER NOW!"

If the bus pulled over, we'd be saved. But the bus doesn't pull over. It goes faster, swerving from side to side.

I'm gripping Sam's left hand. She waves her right hand wildly. I catch it. So now I have both hands, which is good. I squeeze Sam's wrists. But I can't hold on. I can't—

It's like my body tells me what to do. I plant the

toes of my sneakers on the floor behind me. I start walking them back, step-by-step, scooting my body backward a couple of inches at a time. Maybe I can—

Yes!

Half of Sam's head appears over the ledge of the door. It's like I'm a doctor in an emergency room and Sam is a baby I'm trying to deliver. Onto the bus.

I keep wriggling backward. My feet tiptoe into the aisle. That brings Sam's whole head up. Her glasses fall off. But I can't worry about that now.

I keep going until Sam is halfway on the bus. Then I press my hands down hard on her shoulders so she won't fall back out. I push myself to my knees.

We're not going to die!

I sit on the seat and pull her up next to me, shoving her lunch box and backpack out of the way. Then I twist her around so she's sitting on the aisle side, and I'm sitting by the open door.

We just sit, silently, for a few seconds. Not that you can tell we're being quiet, with that cop siren wailing in our ears and the cop on the microphone ordering us to pull over and the blue and red lights flashing around the bus like we're inside a Christmas tree.

Sam shivers all over. Her teeth chatter. Her lips look blue.

I look around for her coat. Then I remember that I lost her coat. And freezing air keeps blowing in through the open door.

I take off my denim jacket and drape it around her little shoulders.

Why am I so wet? Oh, I get it. I'm drenched in sweat.

"Well," I tell her, "now you see what the emergency door is for."

Sam doesn't laugh. But I do. In fact, I giggle so hysterically that I'm sure I'm having a nervous breakdown.

I can't stop laughing. Really. They're going to have to put me in the hospital. People will come from miles around to see Laughing Freddy.

Sam looks at me in amazement. Well, that's good. Maybe my nervous breakdown will help snap her out of *her* nervous breakdown. Ha-ha-ha-ha-ha-ha-ha-ha-ha—

Ooo—that stopped my laughter fast.

The bus turns left so sharply that—

The two wheels on the right side lift up into the air!

The bus is doing a wheelie!

Every kid on the bus screams at the top of their lungs because—

We're turning in front of—

A big brown Benson's Bakery van!

Horns scream. Wheels scream. Brakes scream. I scream. The van comes so close I can see the horrified face of the driver. He spins the wheel.

But he doesn't hit us. He hits the cop car.

No, he didn't, either. The cruiser and the van are jammed right up against each other. They came *that* close to smashing into each other headfirst. But they both stopped just in time.

The bus rockets away, leaving the cops and the bakery van in the dust.

"Yes!" Frank yells. "George! You're brilliant! You lost them!"

It's true. The siren grows softer and softer as the bus zooms ahead. We lost the cops.

At first, I feel awful. But then when I think about it, I feel better.

"This is good," I whisper to Sam.

"This is good?" she repeats, like I'm insane.

"Yeah, it's good they lost the cops. This way they can let us all go."

"This is good," Sam repeats, like she's trying to make herself believe it. "This is great."

I peek over Sam's head. We're zipping along this little nothing of a road. The road runs alongside the interstate, only down below. We thunder past this long cement wall of arches that holds up the highway above us.

From down here you can see some of the trucks going by up on the highway. Weeds grow everywhere. Graffiti scrawls cover the cement arches. But there are no cars. None. And now—

The bus slows down.

I feel like I do when I've been on a scary ride at an amusement park that goes on a lot longer than I would like. The ride is finally over.

Sam grins at me. She throws out her little arms and hugs me. I hug her back.

The bus drives slowly enough for me to shut and lock the emergency door. Finally.

Then the bus parks.

Thank you. Thank you. Thank you.

Everyone gets real quiet.

I feel so relieved. But should I feel relieved?

I just had a bad thought. What if our emergency isn't over? What if we're just on pause? What if things are about to get worse?

I don't know how they could, but maybe—

I hear the two robbers arguing. They keep their voices low. But I catch the word *hostage*.

I lean forward in my seat, straining to hear. From what I can tell, Frank doesn't want to take any hostages. George wants to take one hostage, just to be safe, in case the cops show up again. I feel like raising my hand and trying to help Frank win the argument.

Oops. I guess I must have stuck my head up over the seat because—

"We're thinking about taking a hostage, bright boy," George tells me. "Keep pushing your luck and it's going to be you."

Instead of raising my hand, I drop my head so fast I bump it on the seat ahead of us.

The robbers argue more. Then George yells, "Okay, listen up, kiddies. I know you'd like to stick around for the rest of the ride, but we're going to have to let you off here."

Yes! Frank won the argument! I want to fall on my knees and kiss the grimy metal floor.

"I want this done in an orderly fashion," yells George, "and I want it done fast. Don't make me mad, kiddies, because you're very close to being free."

Free. That has a nice ring to it.

As George opens the bus door I see the big red stop sign stick out on the other side. George sits back, waiting for us to get off. Just like Mr. Dickerson, except with a mask and a gun and two huge black garbage bags of money at his feet.

"Okay," Frank tells us, clapping his hands and jumping up and down. "You heard George! Move it! Move it! Move it!"

I guess you learn more at school than you think. You know how they always drum into you this stuff about single file and being quiet during fire drills? No one ever listens, right? Well, now everyone does it without being asked. We go single file. Silent. Fast.

I'm so excited. I can't believe it. We made it! I'm going to live to be thirteen. And Sam—Sam will live to be six.

I step into the aisle. I wait for Sam as she picks up her backpack and lunch box. I smile at her, a tight little smile. She beams back. Once she's standing behind me in the aisle, I start forward.

We're coming close to the front of the bus. There stands Frank, right next to George, who's behind the wheel. I put my head down. I don't see any reason to look the robbers in the eye. Like maybe they'll think I'm memorizing their eye color.

Outside, kids fall to the ground, they're so relieved.

All Sam and I have to do is walk past the robbers and we'll be outside . . . we'll be free . . .

There isn't much room in the aisle. When I walk past Frank, my elbow brushes against his sweater. It gives me the creeps. Like I just got cooties for all time.

But it's not Frank who really really scares me. It's George. Sitting behind the wheel. I can feel him watching me.

"Hey, kid," he says.

I don't look up. I'm too terrified.

"You were *that* close," he tells me.

Out of the corner of my eye I see George hold up two fingers close together. I know what he means, too. I was that close to ticking him off so much he explodes.

I turn and hold out my hand to Sam.

But Sam just stands there, blocking the whole aisle.

"Go!" Frank yells at her.

My heart stops. Not this again!

"Sam?" I say.

She turns and pushes past the kids who wait behind her. She heads back down the aisle! What is she doing? She's going the wrong way!

"Sam!"

I start back after her, but George claps his hand down on my shoulder.

"But—" I say.

George shoves.

I fall backward and step dowwwnnnn—

Wow, the floor of the bus is about a foot lower than it should beeee—

No, you know what happened? I stepped down onto the first step off the bus. Then I fell down steps two and three. My head smacked the frozen ground outside.

Well, I didn't see stars. But I did see a bright light, like a lightning bolt zigzagged down through my brain.

Someone helps me up. I don't know who.

More kids stream off the bus. They all look scared. No one is doing any celebrating, that's for sure. No one is talking, even.

I make my way through the crowd. I try to follow Sam as she moves back through the bus. Sam—Sam—what are you doing?! Why did you turn back? *Why?*

I jump up and down, waving at her.

Finally, about halfway down the aisle, she stops. She disappears. Then she's back. She now holds her rabbit doll along with my backpack and my skateboard and her backpack and her lunch box. So that's why— She went back for the doll! Of all the stupid—

It's a lot of stuff for her to carry. She smiles at me, though. Very proud.

My hands clutch the sides of my face, like they're somebody else's hands and I have no control over them. I'm so scared. I wave wildly at Sam, pointing to the front of the bus and going, "Off! Off!"

Sam can't wave with her hands full. She turns and joins the crowd filing off. Now she's at the end of the line. I work my way back the other way, following her. Sometimes all I can see is that little ponytail of hers, sticking up like a feather.

Somebody stops me. And hugs me.

I try to get away.

But it's two people. Betsy and Anna. Betsy cries and shakes and it's like she's talking except barely any sound comes out. I hear a lot of "Oh, Freddy."

I hold Betsy's shoulders and give her a little smile as I move her away from me. "It's going to be okay," I say.

Then Anna's arms open wide and fly around my neck. The hug feels great.

I hurry to the bus door. I get there just as Sam does. She's the only kid left on the bus. She gives me a big grin.

Then she drops everything—my backpack, her backpack, her lunch box, her rabbit doll, and my skateboard.

The two backpacks, the bunny, and the lunch box all stay inside the bus. The skateboard bounces and rolls down the steps. I reach down and pick it up. Then I reach for Sam as—

George closes the doors.

And the bus pulls out.

CHAPTER 23

I GUESS THE OTHER KIDS DON'T KNOW THAT SAM IS still on the bus. Because this huge cheer goes up.

It's like the very last day of school. Only there's even more excitement. Kids cry, laugh, shout, jump up and down, hug each other, throw their books high in the air.

I shout, "SAM!" as I run alongside the bus.

I feel like I have this huge hole in my gut. Like Sam is part of me and she just got ripped out. Everything good that happened, everyone getting off the bus, everyone being saved—

It doesn't mean anything because—

"SAM!"

With my free hand, I slap the bus as it goes by. Like that will do anything.

And then I realize what's in my other hand.

The skateboard.

I drop it onto the street and jump onto it, kicking off as the bus goes by. Kick, kick, kick!

The back of the bus slowly pulls away from me.

I have to bend over and reach way out for the bumper. I reach—reach—

Got it! I grab the underside of the bumper with both hands. Then I go into a deeper crouch to keep my balance as—

The bus picks up speed.

CHAPTER 24

WHAT AM I DOING?

I've seen lots of kids pull this tailgating stunt on their bikes or their skateboards or their Rollerblades. Just for a blast. But I've never tried it. I've never even thought about trying it. I hear it's an excellent way to break your neck. Well, I have no interest—zero—in breaking my—

OOOOOH—the bus is going faster.

Faster.

My fingers hurt from hanging on to the metal. But I can't let go. I can't let go. Because Sam—

The red taillights flash in my eyes. Wait a minute! These are brake lights. Is the bus stopping? Please tell me the bus is stopping!

No. The bus isn't stopping. It's *turning*. No!!!

I hang on desperately. I try to turn along with the bus but—

Hmm. A very bad thing is happening. The skateboard is inching farther and farther away from the bus. I try to pull the board back with my legs. Instead—

I let out a low moan as the skateboard moves even farther away. And farther.

Until I'm stretched straight out—

Facedown to the speeding street below.

CHAPTER 25

H<small>ANG ON, FREDDY!</small> I <small>SHOUT AT MYSELF.</small> HANG ON!

And then those red lights flash in my eyes again. The bus slows down a little. I pull myself back up into a crouch. Then the bus slows down some more. And some more.

Could it be?

Yes!

Now the bus is stopping.

I wait until the bus comes to a full halt. I look up. Right over my head I see a green street sign. Washington Street. So this is where they were headed all along. But why? I have no idea.

As quietly as I can, I open the emergency door in back of the bus.

I open the door a little bit at a time.

I don't see the robbers.

They must be up front.

Slowly, I climb inside.

Then—slowly slowly—I stick my head above the seat and peek.

I almost throw up.

CHAPTER 26

THE BUS IS EMPTY.
Sam and the robbers are gone!

CHAPTER 27

I RUN DOWN THE AISLE OF THE BUS.

Then I see them.

The robbers.

They're running up the street, lugging their garbage bags. One of them—it must be George—carries Sam under his arm like a package.

Parked about twenty yards up ahead is a blue Chevy. George shoves Sam in back. Then both robbers jump in the front with their big bags of money.

So that's it! This was their plan all along! To drive out here to the middle of nowhere and switch cars so the cops won't know what car to follow.

This time their car starts perfectly. The blue Chevy drives away. And as they drive off, the robbers toss their masks out the window.

I'm frantic. I'm hopping up and down and grunting and sweating and—

I look around for something, anything, that can help me stop the robbers.

I see some things lying on the floor that look weirdly familiar. So familiar that it takes me a second to realize what they are.

My backpack. Sam's backpack. And Sam's *Kickboxing Kangaroos* lunch box. Nothing that can help me. I keep turning, looking.

Then I see the driver's seat. The keys to the bus hang from the ignition key. . . .

Then it hits me. What I need is all around me. I've got the bus.

CHAPTER 28

I JUMP INTO THE DRIVER'S SEAT. MY FEET BARELY REACH the pedals. I scoot down to the edge of the seat. I slide down.

Then I stare at the keys in the ignition.

It's not like I've never driven before. I've driven. It's just that I've only driven once.

This friend of mine, Alan Davis? Well, his older brother, Billy Davis, he's sixteen. And once he let me and Alan drive his old Mustang around the Giant supermarket parking lot after dark.

I didn't actually make it *around* the parking lot. I hit a shopping cart over in Section B. But I learned the basics.

I'm stalling again. I'm wasting time.

I can do this, I tell myself. I CAN DO THIS!

But that feels like the biggest lie I have ever uttered.

And the blue Chevy is almost out of sight.

I pump the gas once, then turn the ignition. And sure enough the engine turns over and chugs to life.

Then I stare down at the gas pedal. At least I think that's the gas pedal. I don't really remember which pedal is which.

I'm wasting time. I'M WASTING TIME!

And suddenly I'm beyond mad. I'm FURIOUS. Because while I sit here worrying and fretting and fussing, Sam gets farther and farther away.

All my life, I've arrived ten minutes late for everything, just like Mom and Dad always say.

Mr. Late.

Well, if I arrive late this time . . .

"No!" I tell myself. I say it out loud. "Not this time."

Then I pull on the gear lever until the arrow points to R for Ride.

I step on the gas.

CHAPTER 29

OH NO!!!

The bus leaps backward!

I hit the brakes. Hard.

Nope, I must have hit the gas again! Because I'm going backward even faster—

I turn and look behind me and—

I'm going off the road!!

In one more second I'm going to smash into the stone arch that supports the highway—

I hit the brakes. The bus stops. I sit there shaking.

R stands for something else, I now remember. For some reason, R stands for Backward. D must be for Forward. What a stupid system! Stupid, stupid, stupid!

I move the gear stick so the arrow points to D. I hit the gas again. I zoom down the street, screaming my head off.

I'm very scared. Sweat pours out of my face.

But I'm angry, too. It's probably good that I'm so angry or I wouldn't be able to do this because—

I'm driving the bus! I'm driving the bus!

I'm not driving very well, let me tell you.

I can't make the stupid bus go straight.

It keeps turning and—

I keep turning the wheel but—

It's like the bus is going crazy.

I can't keep the bus inside the dotted lines that mark my lane.

Back and forth and back and forth. Like all the bus wants to do is dive to its death off the side of the road.

Every half second I hit the brakes. That means the bus starts and stops along with going back and forth. So I'm getting whiplash in four directions at once.

Every time I jump on the brakes, they make this horrible grinding sound. Like I'm stabbing them or something. That can't be good for the brakes, can it?

But I can't stop jumping on the brakes. Again and again.

Hey. Wait a minute. Look at this. If I don't turn the wheel so much, and if I don't hit the brakes so much, the bus goes straight and smooth.

"Yes!" I shout.

But right away the bus veers off the road again.

But I just have to turn the wheel a little bit and . . .

I shout again.

Now I'm really driving!

Then I realizing something. I can't see the blue Chevy up ahead.

Oh no. Oh no.

They got away.

But maybe they're around the next bend. . . .

Or the next . . .

Or—

A thunder of wings drones overhead. What's that? Sounds like a bird the size of the Empire State Building.

I lean forward and peer up through the windshield.

Hey—it's a chopper!

All right! Must be the cops! I honk the horn. I wave. It's about time. Where have you been?

The helicopter dips, turns, disappears.

I'm still on Washington Street, wherever that is. There are roads leading off this road, of course. Every time I pass a turnoff I twist in my seat and look.

Oh, yeah, like I'm going to see the robbers.

This is totally hopeless. They could have turned anytime. I lost them. I lost them.

Then I see them.

Way down the road.

The blue Chevy.

Chugging along.

I push down harder on the gas. I have to stand on the pedal.

But the lucky thing is, the blue car isn't going that fast.

That puzzles me.

If you rob a bank, don't you drive away fast?

They sure drove fast when they were on the bus.

Then I remember something else. The way the robbers didn't run when they came out of the bank. They walked. That's why so few people even looked at them.

I've got it!

The cops aren't looking for a *blue car*. They're looking for a school bus. So if the robbers don't speed, they won't attract attention.

So there it is.

Well, *I* keep speeding.

I'm gaining on them, too. Now I can see Sam's little head through the back window. From this distance it looks *really* tiny.

I'm so happy to see her, even the back of her head. To see she's okay. Yes!

I'm coming, Sam. I'm coming!

I'll tell you something about Washington Street. It isn't a well-paved road. Potholes everywhere. Seems like I hit every hole. I'm bouncing up and down like I'm inside a popcorn popper. And—

BANG!

I hit a really bad one and the bus shoots to the left.

I hit the brakes to slow down and—

Oh no . . . Ohhhh NO!!!

The bus isn't slowing down!

I jump onto the brake pedal with all my might.

The pedal goes right down to the floor.

The bus doesn't stop.

Doesn't slow down even slightly.

I wrecked the brakes!

CHAPTER 30

OH NO OH NO OH NO OH NO.

The brakes are gone.

The brakes are gone the brakes are gone the brakes—

Get a grip on yourself, Freddy. It's not so bad if the brakes are gone. You don't need to stop right now. You're trying to catch Sam. Remember? If the gas pedal broke, you'd be in real trouble.

I go around another bend.

And way up ahead I see—

Two cop cars with flashing lights. Parked by the side of the road.

The cops found the robbers! The cops found the robbers! I'm saved! Sam's saved! *We're* saved!

I'm so excited I'm bouncing up and down in my seat.

The blue car drives slowly toward the cop cars. Closer. Closer.

And—
What?
The blue car drives *past* the cop cars.
And the cops make no move to stop it.

CHAPTER 31

MY JAW DROPS. WHY WOULD THEY LET THE ROBBERS go by? Are they insane? What are they thinking about?

Suddenly the cop cars pull out, blocking the road. Doors fly open. Cops pile out. They take up these scary, army positions—legs apart, arms straight out, two hands on their guns. They're all aiming—

At me.

Now I get it.

I'm driving the bus.

The helicopter spotted *me*.

They think I'm—

CHAPTER 32

"**DON'T SHOOT!**" I SCREAM. "**IT'S ME! FREDDY!**"

I speed toward the cops. I can't stop. No brakes. Any second now I'm going to hear POP POP POP and little holes will dot my chest like Swiss cheese.

But no—no—

I guess they can see it's just me in the bus, because they're lowering their guns.

And now they're diving in all directions as—

SMASH!

I crash right through the cop cars, turning them aside like swinging doors.

"CAN'T STOP!" I yelled.

But I guess they already figured that out.

I race ahead.

Okay, Freddy. You're on your own again. No cops to help you. It's up to you, kid.

I stand on the gas pedal.

The road curves.

Curves are hard. You've got to turn the wheel a little, then a little more, and then a little more.

I scream during curves.

But up ahead I see the blue car again.

Oh no.

The blue car is turning left.

I haven't tried a turn yet.

This ought to be fun.

I turn left.

Well, I just learned something else about driving.

It's important to slow down when you turn.

Because otherwise the whole bus tips onto two wheels.

Wow. This wheelie wasn't like the last wheelie the bus did. That first one was a tiny tip. This time I was driving sideways for a second. And it was fifty-fifty which way the bus was going to go.

Up ahead, the blue car turns again. Great.

But this time I've got a little more time to plan.

I can't slow down. No brakes. But I figure I can make a longer, slower turn by cutting across the lawn of that old weather-beaten house on the corner.

Here we go. . . .

I'm driving over the lawn.

Past the house.

And—

There's a clothesline! There's a clothesline! And there's a woman standing right behind it folding her wash into—

SNAP!

The bus hits the clothesline.

Out of the corner of my eye I see this white pole that held one end of the clothesline come flying out of the ground.

Then I see the woman throw her laundry basket up in the air.

And then I hear the dull thud as the bus smacks something soft. And—

I see the different parts of the woman's body—her legs, her arms—all splat against the windshield.

CHAPTER 33

WAIT A MINUTE! OH, WOW! I DIDN'T HIT THE WOMAN at all, I only hit the laundry basket. The windshield is covered with *clothes*!

HA-HA-HA-HA-HA-HA! I'm screaming with happiness and relief. 'Cause in my rearview mirror I can see that woman. She's still alive. She's got her hands over her mouth. She looks horrified.

She seems to be worried about where I'm going.

You know, it's probably not such a good idea to be speeding across some yard and not be able to see where I'm headed.

But I have no idea how to get all this laundry off the windshield.

There's this whole panel of buttons on the left side of the dash. But I don't have time to look for the switch for the windshield wipers.

Oh, that was bright.

I just yanked on the door handle, like that would do something.

All it did was open the big red stop sign next to my ear.

Oh, thank you, wind! Thank you!

The wind caught those clothes and blew them off the windshield.

I can see again.

I can see that I'm about to drive into a house.

CHAPTER 34

I TURN THE WHEEL AS HARD AS I CAN.

I ride the brake, even though that does nothing.

And I miss the house.

Not by much. But I miss it.

Instead, I drive straight into the garage.

Everything goes black for a second. Then I smash out the back of the garage with wood blasting everywhere. Pieces of lumber bang the windshield.

The bus races on.

And now I sort of get my bearings and I can see where I'm going. Across another lawn. Past another house. Another.

Every time I go past a house I catch another peek at the blue car, out on the road.

I don't know how long I can keep this up. I'm driving across lawns while the Chevy drives on the road. That means I have to steer around bikes and patio furniture and more clotheslines and empty swimming pools and birdhouses and mailboxes and barbecues and parked cars and, of course, more people.

Boy, do they look surprised.

There, I'm off the lawns and back on the road.

Excellent.

The blue Chevy drives fast, trying to lose me. But I keep it in sight.

Soon I stop seeing houses flying by on either side. I only see houses every now and then. And then I smell pine trees. And wet rotting leaves. And then there are more trees all around. And more trees. And—

I know where we're going. Out by the reservoir. Alan Davis and some friends—we all rode our bikes out here last summer. Alan found this old rope and all the guys swung on it and jumped naked into the water. Except me. I was the big chicken. They didn't tease me too much, but I was so embarrassed I rode home without them.

Well, maybe while I'm out here this time I can take a moment to find that rope and jump in the water. Because that sure seems like nothing now. When I compare it with—

But you know what? I'm starting to relax a little. I mean, I'm not having a heart attack *all* the time. I'm still driving really fast. And I still have no brakes. But after driving across lawns, chasing after the blue Chevy on roads is a piece of cake.

I guess anything that goes on long enough you get used to. I'm beginning to feel like I'm playing a video game and I'm in the zone, you know? Things keep flying at me, but if I stay loose I can steer my bus.

And all the time I've got this anger in my mouth like acid. Those robbers! Those robbers!

Sam!

And then—

BUMP BUMP BUMP BUMP

I think my face is going to fall off, we're bumping up and down so much. We're on dirt roads now. They're like the roads we drive on when we go camping. With woods pressing close on either side and branches that keep smacking the windshield like they're trying to hit me. And—

THWACK! A big branch bends back one of the hood mirrors.

Then the blue Chevy turns—

And I follow and—

The woods clear.

Off to one side stands a little old cabin.

That's where the Chevy is headed.

I miss that turn.

Out of the corner of my eye I see the Chevy park by the cabin. I fly on. Straight ahead.

Straight ahead stands—

A rickety old wooden dock. And the dock leads to—

The big gray reservoir, which is covered with a thin sheet of ice.

CHAPTER 35

WELL, IT LOOKS LIKE I'M GOING TO BE DIVING INTO the reservoir after all.

Okay, Freddy, you have a problem.

How do you stop the bus without brakes before you drive off the dock into the reservoir, go through the thin ice, sink, and drown?

It's kind of like the word problems I got stuck on for my math take-home test last night. Except if I get this problem wrong—

I take my foot off the gas. That's for starters. But I don't slow down. I'm halfway to the edge of the lake. And—

I just had a brainstorm. I remembered my first driving mistake. When I set the gears to R for Ride. R turned out to be R for Backward. Maybe if I go forward but the gears go backward, it will come out even and I'll stop and I won't sink and drown.

Hey, it's worth a shot because now I'm about

thirty yards from the dock and rumbling and roaring so fast I—

I squeeze the button on the side of the gear lever and yank the lever down hard, trying to throw the bus into R.

Except the gear stick doesn't want to go into R. I jam it with all my might, which costs me another second.

And now I'm ten yards from the dock and—

I jam harder.

You know what? Emergencies make you stronger. I mean it. If this were an arm-wrestling contest, I think I just pushed hard enough to win a match against Arnold Schwarzenegger. I'm shouting, too. With anger. Like what I'm doing, I'm not pulling on a gear stick. I'm punching that George guy in the nose.

The stick moves. The arrow points to R.

And right away there's this horrible growling sound, like the bus is choking on something.

But the bus doesn't go backward. It keeps rushing forward, right onto the old wooden dock.

And the dock is only about ten yards long.

It leads right into the—

I just thought of something else I can try.

Turn the wheel.

Yes!

See that?

I didn't go straight off the dock into the water.

I went off the side of the dock and—

Ohhhhhhhhhhhhhhhhhhhhhhhhhhhhhhhhhhhhhhhhhhhhhh!

Through the air and—

Whomp!!!

I hit the sandy bank instead of the water and—

I feel all my organs rise up into my throat and then crash back down into their proper places as—

I bounce up the sandy bank into the woods and—

Now there are trees all around me. Little trees and big trees. And—

I steer wildly as I drive up the hill. I avoid a couple of the big trees. I run over a few of the little little trees. And—

Could it be? Yes! The bus is slowing down.

As I go up and up this hill the bus slows down more and more. Why? Because we're going uphill. Yes!

The bus is stopping. This is great. *How to Stop a Bus with No Brakes*. By Fred C. Evans. Just drive up a—

Wait a minute.

Is the bus . . . ?

Yes, the bus rolls *down*hill and—

BAM!!

You know what?

It's probably a good thing I just bashed the rear end of the bus into that big tree. Because at least I stopped the bus.

That's good news. Except—

I just looked in my overhead mirror.

One of the robbers is making his way along the sandy bank. Headed this way.

Okay. This is what you wanted, Freddy. You wanted to have it out with these guys. Well, here's your chance.

Except as angry as I am, now I'm so scared I want to weep.

The robber has his mask off. I wonder which robber that is. George or Frank?

Well, I guess it doesn't matter.

Whoever it is, he has his gun.

CHAPTER 36

OKAY. HERE'S A NEW PROBLEM. MAN. GUN. ME.

Go, Freddy! Five seconds. Solve it!

Okay, let's see. I can get off the bus and run for it. Bad plan. I can't run faster than a bullet. I can't run as fast as most of the kids in my class. Right now I don't even know if I can walk. Too scared!

I need a weapon. I look around. All I see are two backpacks and Sam's lunch box.

The robber leaves the sandy bank, starts into the woods.

I scramble out of the driver's seat and pick up the lunch box. I open it. My choice of weapons is—

1) A peanut-butter-and-jelly sandwich.

2) An apple.

3) A tiny carton of orange juice with a straw attached.

4) A plastic baggy with three chocolate-chip cookies.

Not very good weapons unless I shove them all down the robber's throat and choke him.

Out the back window I can see the robber making his way closer, closer.

I look down at the lunch box.

Then it hits me.

The perfect weapon is staring me right in the face.

I CLOSE THE LUNCH BOX AND SNAP THE SNAPS. NOW I need a hiding place.

I whirl around, gaping at the bus. I have no idea where to hide. I crouch down as I make my way through the bus.

Then I stop. I see something black and shiny lying on the floor under one of the seats.

A gun!

What?!

I almost scream.

Then I remember. Jay's water pistol.

So now I have two weapons.

Two weapons but no hiding place. I run back up to the front of the bus. I'm getting to be like Frank. Running up and down the aisle. I stand in the front of the bus, panting like a dog.

The robber is twenty yards from the back of the bus.

I HAVE NO TIME TO THINK!

That's all I'm thinking. How I have no time to think. And—

Why is that little shaft of sunlight drilling down onto my face?

I look up.

CHAPTER 38

A HIDING PLACE! A HIDING PLACE!

One that Sam pointed out to me!

I have to move fast. No time to think.

There.

Made it. Just as—

The robber reaches the back of the bus. He starts around the side of the bus. He heads for the front door.

I can see the top of the robber's head and his body through the windows. It looks like a filmstrip, because I see him in all these different window frames, one after another.

I hear the robber pry open the bus door. Hear him walk on.

Then the footsteps stop.

He must be surprised that I'm not here. "GEORGE!" he screams. "HE'S GONE!"

So now I know who it is. Frank. Good. I'm less

scared of Frank than I am of George. Of course, I'm so scared of both of them it doesn't really matter, but—

"HE'S PROBABLY HIDING BEHIND ONE OF THE SEATS!" George yells back. "LOOK AROUND."

Frank's footsteps start down the aisle. He goes right past my hiding place.

What's the matter with me? There was my chance. There was my chance. It came and it went. Now it's gone. I froze. I froze I froze I froze.

"Hey, kid, come out, would ya?" Frank asks. "Don't give me any more trouble. I'm having a really bad day."

You're having a bad day?

My heart pounds. I can hear it. Boom. Boom.

I hope Frank can't hear it because he's coming closer and closer and—

Well, Freddy. Here's another case when you have to be right on time. You can't freeze. You can't be ten minutes late. You can't even be one tenth of a tenth of a second late.

I wait until Frank is right underneath me.

Then I swing down from the overhead emergency door and smash him with all my might with Sam's lunch box.

CHAPTER 39

FRANK SWAYS SLIGHTLY.
I smack him again.
Down he goes with a moan.
I jump down. My plan is to grab his gun.
But instead—
GEORGE GRABS *ME*!

CHAPTER 40

GEORGE!

While I was busy studying the top of Frank's head and waiting for just the right second to bonk him, George must have boarded the bus.

He grabs me by the scruff of the neck. He yanks me toward him. He doesn't have his mask on. I recognize him by his dark, angry eyes.

He holds my shirt tight, choking me.

I wait to die.

"Freddy!"

It's Sam. She climbs onto the bus right behind George. Hi, Sam. But I have no breath and no voice. George holds my shirt too tight. So I can't really speak with her at the moment.

"You leave him alone!" Sam screams at George.

This isn't what I was planning. I was going to chase after Sam and protect her. And once again that little five-year-old is trying to protect *me*.

Sam throws herself at George. He lets me go, shoving me down the aisle of the bus. Then he shoves Sam. She ends up in the driver's seat.

"Sam," I say. I want to yell, but I'm too scared. It's like I'm whispering from the bottom of the reservoir. "Just go. Run. Run for your life."

Sam doesn't go.

George has his gun stuck in the belt of his pants. It's hard not to keep looking at it. "Do you have any idea," George says, grinding out the words, "how much trouble you've caused me?"

I think about that. Like I've got to give him an answer.

George shakes his head slowly from side to side. "What am I going to do with you, kid?"

That's something my father always says, when he's really mad at me. Except the things my father thinks up to do to me are usually things like grounding me for a week. Somehow I don't think that's what George has in mind.

George looks down. He's looking at what I have in my hands. He laughs. "You think you're going to stop me with a water pistol, kid?"

Jay fooled me with his water pistol. I guess I thought maybe I cold fool the robbers. Wrong.

But then I realize something else I could use the water pistol for.

I pull the trigger. I squirt George right in the eye.

It doesn't have the big effect I was hoping for. George grabs for me with both hands.

Time to use my other weapon. The lunch box. I swing for his head.

I miss.

But the lunch box opens. So out comes the peanut-butter-and-jelly sandwich, the apple, the carton of orange juice, and the baggy of cookies. All the food flies at George's head.

I was right. Cookies and juice aren't great weapons. George just looks madder. I turn and run straight down the aisle. I fling open the emergency door in the very back of the bus and jump.

George jumps off the bus right after me.

I cut around the back of the bus. I figure that will throw him off the track.

George cuts right with me.

I keep running. Up the other side of the bus.

I get as far as the hood of the bus when George's hand grabs my shirt.

CHAPTER 41

CLANG!

George lets go of me.

Slowly, I turn.

I expect to see George's mean face snarling down at me.

I don't see him at all.

I look down.

George kneels on the ground, holding his face with both hands.

I look up.

Over George's head is the big red stop sign that sticks out from the side of the bus.

Sam sits in the driver's seat.

That little genius!

She must have closed and opened the bus door! She opened that big stop sign right in the robber's face!

He sure stopped.

And now his hands drop and he—
Falls slowly—
Face down into the—
Frozen ground.
Out.
Cold.

CHAPTER 42

THINGS ARE HAPPENING SO FAST. IT FEELS LIKE LIFE IS spinning all around us like a tornado. And Sam and I—

Sam and I move slowly through it all in a daze.

First the helicopter zooms overhead. Then cops arrive from all directions. Sirens. Spinning lights. The cops handcuff the robbers. Other cops put blankets around me and Sam.

Frank sobs as they lead him away, "Please, please don't call my mother!"

I hope they're calling his mother right this second.

This big beefy cop grins and pounds me on the back. "You did some job out there, kid," he tells me. "Some job!"

Then this woman cop puts us in the back of a cruiser. We're alone. I grin at Sam.

Sam doesn't smile back. Instead, she starts crying. And when she starts crying, I start crying. Like suddenly all the tension of the day gets to me. And then we're hugging each other. Holding on to each other real hard.

After we cry for a while and hug for a while, we just sit quietly. I guess this is what they mean when they talk about being in shock. Sam gets a hold of my hand and won't let go. Like she's afraid she's going to get separated from me again. I squeeze back every now and then to tell her she doesn't have to worry.

But as it turns out, she does have to worry. Because they take us to the hospital. (Not that anything is wrong with us. Just to be safe and check us out.) And all the kids from the bus are there. And everyone is shouting and hugging. I keep looking for Sam, but I keep getting swept away from her.

These doctors and nurses come and they've got clipboards and stethoscopes. They lead us into little examining rooms to ask us questions and check us out.

And then, I don't know how much later it is, but we're all back in the lobby. And here come the parents. They rush in crying and hugging us.

I don't see *my* parents. Ha! I guess they're the late ones this time!

Oh, but here's Mr. and Mrs. Hatchett. They hug Sam for about ten minutes each. Then they come rushing over and hug me and thank me for all I did. I smile at Sam. She holds her hand out to me, but—

More cops come and all these reporters and everyone's clapping me on the back. Or just putting their hands on me. Like I'm some TV star and they want to be able to say they touched me and—

You know? It's finally starting to sink in. I really did do a great thing this morning!

"Freddy! Over here!"

All these photographers, snapping pictures of me. Flash! Flash!

And there's Sam.

Her parents are leading her away. She looks back at me. Like she's sad. She keeps turning back.

"Freddy! Come on, boy. Look at the camera. That's it. Give us a smile!"

I smile for the cameras and—

I let Sam go.

CHAPTER 43

WHAT AM I DOING?

I didn't come all this way to blow it now.

The hard part is over. I'm flunking the easy part.

"Excuse me—" I say. I run across the hospital lobby.

"Hey! Freddy! Where are you going! C'mon! Don't be like that! We need your picture, son!"

I grab Sam from behind. She squeals as I pick her up and swing her through the air.

"Hey, Freddy," Mr. Hatchett says, turning red, "Sam's had kind of a rough morning. We want to take her home."

"In a sec," I say.

I hoist Sam up, up, up till she sits on my shoulders. I think I just got a hernia doing it, too. But I march her back to the photographers and now I'm really smiling. "Go ahead," I say. "Take as many pictures as you like."

And you know what?

Right now?

I think this is the best I've ever felt in my entire life.

And—

You know what? I'm going to make a promise to myself.

Right here and now.

Freddy Evans, you are never ever going to be late for an appointment again.

CHAPTER 44

I'M RUNNING. DOWN MY DRIVEWAY. I'VE GOT MY skateboard in one hand and a hot pizza bagel (my breakfast!) in the other.

I'm going to catch the bus! I'm going to catch the bus!

There. Made it to the end of the drive with—

Let's see.

A whole minute left. Not bad. I take a big bite of pizza bagel and burn off the roof of my mouth.

Ow!

It's been three weeks since the robbers took over Elmsford Bus #109. And so far I've been true to my word. I haven't missed the bus once. Okay, I came close a couple of times. Okay, I came close every time. But—

It's been some three weeks, let me tell you.

That first couple of nights the phone rang off the

wall with reporters asking me questions. Maybe you saw me on the news. "Kid Hero Drives Bus."

I was famous. At least for a day or two.

Mr. Janusonis, our school principal, he made everyone who was on the bus go to these daily group counseling sessions. We sat around in a circle and talked about our feelings. Were kids treating us strangely in school? Were we having bad dreams? That kind of stuff. I kind of liked it except for one thing. Sam's parents didn't let her come to any of the sessions.

They won't let her come out and play on the street after school, either, unless they're right there to watch her. I guess they feel guilty for letting her ride the bus alone that morning. But I think they're overdoing it.

Every night I call Sam and tell her I'll see her on the bus tomorrow. She always laughs, but she never shows up.

Well, she's got about thirty seconds left if she's planning on taking the bus this morning.

Twenty.

Nineteen.

Wow. Two things just happened at once. One is really good and one is really bad.

The really good thing is, I see Sam walking down the street toward me, with her lunch box and her bunny rabbit! She's waving and grinning, and I'm waving and grinning back. I'm so excited.

Yes!

But at the same time I hear this high-pitched beeping coming from our house.

That can't be the burglar alarm. I punched in the number so carefully.

And besides, the burglar alarm sounds a lot louder than this.

No, it's not the burglar alarm. You know what it is? It's the smoke detector. And that means—

I forgot to turn off the oven after I cooked my pizza bagels! I'm about to burn down the house! And—

Wouldn't you know it. Here comes the bus. The new yellow one we got to replace the one that I drove.

No!

Sam is running toward me.

Mr. Dickerson honks.

I look up at the house.

I've got about thirty seconds to run back to the house and turn off the stove so I don't miss Sam and the bus.

I think I can make it. . . .